DEAR Riley

WORDS CANNOT EXPRESS HOW SPECIAL YOU ARE.
BUT HERE ARE TWENTY-SIX THAT TRY! EACH
ONE SO PERFECTLY DESCRIBES YOU.
YOU ARE ALL OF THESE WONDERFUL
QUALITIES AND SO MUCH MORE.

LOVE

We love you so... We love to watch you learn and Grow. This Special book is all
about you... we are so proud of all that do! love, mom & dad

A IS FOR AMAZING,

THAT'S RILEY

IN EVERY WAY!

B IS FOR THE

SPECIAL WAY

YOU BRIGHTEN UP

EACH DAY.

B

C IS FOR YOUR COURAGE. YOU DON'T FEAR OF WHAT YOU DOING.

D IS FOR YOUR DARING. YOU ALWAYS CARRY THROUGH.

E IS FOR YOUR ENERGY, SO VIBRANT AND SO BRIGHT !

F IS FOR FOREVER

YOU HAVE MY

LOVE

FOREVER

G IS FOR GIFT

YOU ARE A PERFECT GIFT TO ME BY THE UNIVERSE

MY SON,
YOU ARE MY
HEART

MY SON

YOU ARE MY INSPIRATION

J IS FOR JUMP

THOSE WHO DON'T JUMP WILL NEVER FLY

K IS FOR KING
YOU ARE THE
KING OF
MY HEART

L IS FOR

LEARN

FAILLURE

IS A SUCCESS IF

WE LEARN

FROM IT

YOU LEARN SO MUCH FROM MAKING MISTAKES

THE BEST PARTS
OF YOUR FATHER
ARE THE BEST PARTS OF YOU.
NEVER

FORGET WHERE
YOU CAME FROM

YOU ARE THE OBEDIENT SON

P IS FOR PARACHUTES

MINDS ARE LIKE PARACHUTES, THEY ONLY FUNCTION WHEN THEY ARE OPEN.

YOU'RE THE WATER
THAT QUENCHES MY THIRST
AND BREAD THAT SATISFIES
MY HUNGER. YOU ARE
EVERYTHING,
MY BABY.

You are the

Reason

for my

Happiness

THE BEAUTIFUL THING ABOUT LEARNING IS NOBODY CAN TAKE IT AWAY FROM YOU.

U IS FOR UNIQUE

ALWAYS REMEMBER

THAT YOU ARE

ABSOLUTELY

UNIQUE

V IS FOR VACATION
LOTS OF PLACES TO
SEE . . .
I LOVE TO GO
EXPLORING,
WITH MY FAMILY

YOU ARE EVERYTHING
I NEED TO
SURVIVE IN THIS
WORLD

X IS FOR

XOXO

FOR ALL THE LOVE...
MY FAMILY IS SO
HAPPY I WAS SENT
HERE FROM ABOVE

THE REASON FOR MY EXISTENCE IS SIMPLE, IT IS YOU

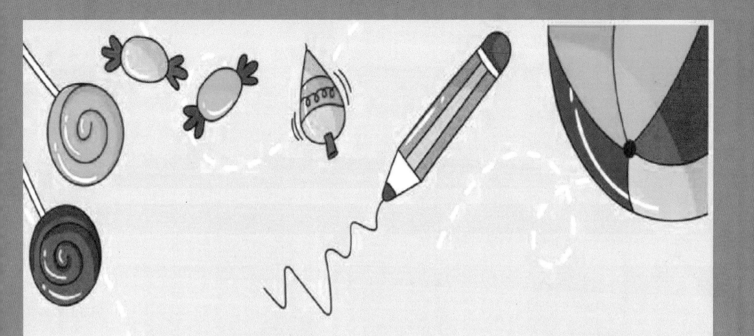

Z IS FOR ZANY

YOU ARE ZANY AND COMICAL.